W9-AXU-876

THE UGLY DUCKLING

story retold by Jim Lawrence • illustrated by Tim Hildebrandt

Modern Publishing
A Division of Unisystems, Inc.
New York, New York 10022

Out in the country, surrounded by green meadows and woods, there was an old stone house that looked like a castle.

How lovely it was there in the summer, with the wheat all golden and the hay in stacks!

A stork walked about the fields stretching his long red legs. He chattered in Egyptian, which he had learned to speak while on his winter travels.

There was water all around the stone house. And on the bank, among the tall leafy weeds, a Mother Duck sat on her nest of eggs.

One day the eggs cracked open and out stepped her little ducklings.

"*Peep, Peep!*" they cried. "*Cheep! Cheep!*"

They tottered about, exploring under the leaves. "Oh, how beautiful the world is!" said the ducklings.

But the biggest egg had yet to hatch. "*Quack, quack!*" said the Mother Duck. "I guess I'll sit a while longer."

An old Granny Duck waddled ashore. "How's your new family?" she asked.

"Fine! Aren't they cute little things?" their Mama beamed fondly. "But this one big egg still hasn't cracked open."

"Hmm, looks to me like a turkey egg," said the old Granny Duck. "I got fooled that way once. When it did hatch, the silly little thing wouldn't go near the water!"

"Oh well, I'll wait a bit longer," said the Mother Duck.

"Suit yourself," quacked Granny as she turned to leave.

At long last, the big egg was hatched. *"Yipe, chirp!"* said the young one inside.

The Mother Duck's heart sank. "Oh my, what a big ugly baby!" she thought.

"Never mind," she told herself. "At least it's no turkey, so it must be mine, and I shall love it like the others. But it had better not be afraid to wet its toes, or I'll push it in the water myself!"

The next day, the Mother Duck led her little brood into the water. "Follow me!" she quacked.

They paddled with their little webbed feet, and soon they were swimming about as well as their Mama.

The big gray one took to the water very well. "How nicely he swims!" thought the Mother Duck. "And he's really not bad-looking, once you get used to him."

Afterward, she took her babies back to the barnyard.

What a noisy place it was! There was loud clucking and squawking and gobbling and honking, as the chickens and ducks, and turkeys and geese squabbled over their food.

A plump Spanish lady duck, approached them. "What a nice family you have, my dear . . . though I must say, that big gray one looks rather odd!"

"He swims well and behaves himself," defended the Mother Duck, smoothing her duckling's feathers with her bill. "I'm sure he'll turn out just fine!"

But the other birds all made fun of the Ugly Duckling.

"Ugh! What a freak!" said a young boy duck. He attacked the gray duckling and pecked at it.

"*Gobble, gobble!* Who brought this thing into our yard?" said a turkey gobbler, puffing out its feathers to scare away the youngster.

His mother tried to protect him, but he was nipped and pecked at and teased by everyone. Even his brothers and sisters made fun of him, and he was kicked away whenever they were fed.

The poor Ugly Duckling was so unhappy he finally ran away.

Although he took a long hop, skip and jump, he barely made it over the hedge around the barnyard. And in doing so, his stubby flapping wings startled all the little birds in the bushes. They flew up and away, chirping with fright.

"I'm so ugly, I scare everyone away," the Ugly Duckling thought sadly.

He blundered and wandered until it grew dark, when he came to the marshes where the wild ducks lived. "Perhaps they will let me stay here," thought the duckling as he lay in the rushes all night, weary and homesick.

The next morning, the Ugly Duckling was awakened as the wild ducks swooped down upon him. "What a strange creature this is!" they quacked. "Who are you?"

The Ugly Duckling tried to bow politely, as his mother had taught him. "I . . . I'm a duck too," he faltered.

At this they all laughed. "That's what you think! . . . Well, we don't care what you call yourself as long as you don't try to join our flock!"

The Ugly Duckling hadn't even dared to hope to join them. All he wanted was to be left alone.

But then, a couple of wild goosey-ganders flew by. "Hey you!" they called. "You're so funny looking, we'd never be seen with you," they laughed.

BANG! BANG! Suddenly, loud, scary noises made it impossible for the Ugly Duckling to hear what the young ganders were saying.

They were being shot at by hunters and the panicked birds quickly flew up from the marshes as a big hairy beast came splashing through the water. Its tongue was out, and its eyes glared. It was one of the hunters' gun-dogs, looking for downed birds.

The Ugly Duckling hid down among the water weeds, scared out of his wits. But the dog swam right past. "Thank goodness I'm so ugly. It knows it wouldn't like the taste of me!" thought the poor duckling.

He waited till everything was clear. Then he scuttled away from the marsh and made his way over the fields.

Toward evening, he came to a little old cottage. It was so weather-beaten and broken-down, the door had even come loose from its hinges, leaving it open a crack.

By now, the wind was blowing so hard that the poor lonely duckling had to squat low to keep from being blown over. "Maybe I can squeeze inside," he thought. And he did.

An old woman lived inside with her cat, Sonny, and her hen, Chickabiddy.

The next morning, the cat meowed and the hen clucked as they noticed the intruder. The old woman came over to see what the fuss was all about. But she didn't see that well and she mistook the Ugly Duckling for a full grown female duck.

"Oh, goody!" she said in her little old voice. "Maybe now we'll have some fine duck eggs to eat!"

But the days passed and there were no eggs. Sonny and Chickabiddy weren't surprised. They had never liked the homely stranger, anyhow. They thought he was intruding and wanted him to go away.

"If the gray thing couldn't lay eggs, or arch its back and purr, what good was it anyhow?" thought Chickabiddy.

The lonely duckling sat in a corner, longing for fresh air and sunshine. He wanted so much to swim in the water that he couldn't stop himself from telling the hen.

"Are you crazy?" clucked Chickabiddy. "Do you suppose Sonny or I or the old woman would ever want to swim in the water? If you can't be as wise as we are, at least be thankful you have a nice, warm, dry place to live!"

At last the duckling could stand it no longer. "I must get out of here," he said.

"Go then," said Chickabiddy. "We'll be glad to get rid of you."

So the duckling went to the water. He swam and floated and dived down deep. But still he was lonely, and no one would have anything to do with him, because he looked so strange.

The seasons changed and autumn set in. The days grew shorter, and the sky turned dark and cloudy. Leaves withered off the trees and were blown about in the wind. A raven perched on a fence and cawed from the cold. The Ugly Duckling shivered sadly.

One evening at sunset, he glimpsed a flock of the most beautiful birds he had ever seen.

They were sparkling white, with long graceful necks and great strong wings. Their cries seemed to pierce his heart as they soared off to warmer lands.

The duckling stretched his own neck and let out a shriek. It sounded so strange, he scared himself! He dived down to the bottom of the lake feeling all mixed up inside.

When he came up again, all he could think of was those lovely white birds. He could never hope to be like them, of course, but he knew he would always love them. Ugly as he was, he would be satisfied if other ducks would just put up with him.

As winter set in, the weather got bitter and cold, and there was very little food for the Ugly Duckling to eat.

Then the lake began to freeze. The poor duckling had to keep swimming around to keep warm.

Finally, he was surrounded by ice. He had to paddle harder and faster to keep the small pool of water that he swam in from freezing. At last he was too weak to move and he quickly froze in the ice.

A peasant found him the next morning. He broke the ice with his wooden shoe and carried the duckling home.

The peasant's wife took care of the poor thing, and in the warm cottage he was soon able to move about again.

The children wanted to play with the Ugly Duckling. But their grabby hands scared him, and he fluttered about wildly—first into the milk pan, then the butter tub, then the flour bin and . . .

What a sight he was! The woman slapped at him, and the children shrieked with laughter. But finally the duckling escaped out the door and flopped down weakly in the snow.

The winter was awful. But, somehow the duckling stayed alive through the hungry, gloomy days and long, dark, freezing nights.

Gradually, the sun grew warmer and the songbirds returned. Birds filled the air and the duckling yearned to fly. He spread his wings and beat the air.

The next thing he knew, he was soaring through the sky!

Oh, how lovely was the spring! He landed on a garden pond where apple trees blossomed overhead and the scent of lilacs filled the air.

Three beautiful white swans came gliding toward him. He was sure they were angry at him for intruding. "Never mind," he thought. "It's better to be attacked and killed by such royal creatures than be teased and pecked at by other birds!"

He bowed his head humbly. Then he saw his own reflection in the water—and let out a cry. He was no longer an ugly gray duckling, but a splendid white swan!